THIS IS THE PLACE FOR ME

by JOANNA COLE

pictures by WILLIAM VAN HORN

SCHOLASTIC INC.

New York Toronto London Auckland Sydney

For Christopher Anthony Lauhoff
—J. C.

For Glen and Esther Van Horn
—W. V. H.

ISBN 0-590-33996-6

Text copyright © 1986 by Joanna Cole.
Illustrations copyright © 1986 by William Van Horn
All rights reserved. Published by Scholastic Inc.
Art direction by Diana Hrisinko
Book design by Sarah McElwain

12 11 10 9 8 7 6 5 4 3 2 1   10   6 7 8 9/8 0 1/9

Morty the bear was always
breaking things in his house.
He was so big, he couldn't help it.

He broke his chair.

He broke his table.

He broke his door.

One night he broke his bedroom window. When he woke
up in the morning, there was snow all over everything.
"This house is a mess! I need a new house," said Morty.

Morty packed his bag.
And he set out to find a new home.

He walked and walked.

He found a cave.

"This is the place for me!" said Morty.

He moved in.

Then he moved out —
FAST!

"I can't live here!" said Morty.
"I have to find another house."

Morty walked and walked.
He found a *very* nice house.

"This is the place for me!" said Morty.

Morty liked his new house.
But late at night, Morty woke up.
He was hungry for a snack.

Before too long the house was...

... all gone!

"That house was delicious," said Morty.
"But now I have to find another one."

Morty walked and walked.

He came to a good house.

"I like this house," he said.

"Oh, oh," Morty said. "This is *not* the place for me."
Morty was too heavy.

He dried himself off.
And went looking
for a house again.

He found one...

but it was too small.

He found another one...

but it was too thin.

He found another...

but it was too scary!

Poor Morty!
He was all alone in the world.
He had no place to live.

He walked along sadly.

Suddenly he stopped.
There was a house.
The door was broken.
The windows were broken.

The table was broken.
The chair was broken.

BUT...

It did *not* have a dragon.
It was *not* too small.
It was *not* too thin.
Morty could not *sink* it.
He could not *eat* it.
And it was *not* scary.

Morty fixed the door.
He fixed the windows.
He fixed the table and chair.
Now the house was as good as new.

"This is the place for me," said Morty.
"It is much better than my old house."